Corolla Wild Horses

"Keep them wild and free!"

Acknowledgements

A special thanks goes out to Niki Schoenfeld, one of the greatest editors ever! I also want to thank the following people whose inspiration and guidance helped to make this book possible: Karen McKalprin, Steve Edwards, and Donna Snow. The Pinnacle Corporation also deserves a word of appreciation for their support, as do my horse-loving friends from the S.O.A.R. Therapeutic Riding Center of Southwest Louisiana: Jeanne Dennis, Heather Dionne, Stacy Verret and Nathalie Miller. You ladies are all heroes! And I would also like to give a heartfelt thanks to my writing buddies: Rose Henny, Linda Lee and Tommie Townsley. I would be remiss if I left out one of the most important persons in the making of this book—Erin Casteel. She has been a delight to work with these past few months! I believe she has a great future ahead of her illustrating children's books. Last, I want to thank my husband Don for his encouragement throughout the years, without which none of this would have been feasible.

Linda Whittington Hurst

To my grandchildren:
Aidan, Elody & Dylan James
~with all my love~
LWH
****
To my mom and dad ~ Erin

Third Edition   3 4 5 6 7 8 9 10

Printed in the USA
Cover design by Joanne Bolton, www.boltonprinting.com

The text for this book is set in Papyrus. The illustrations are rendered in watercolor.

ISBN – 978-0-615-49695-5

e-mail: linda@lindawhurst.com

The Adventures of

Red Feather

Wild Horse of Corolla

by Linda Whittington Hurst

Illustrated by Erin E.I. Casteel

Red Feather was a wild horse. He lived with his herd on the island called the Outer Banks, near the town of Corolla. He was a mahogany bay and he was beautiful—except for one thing— half of his left ear was missing. He lost it in a fight with another wild stallion.

Everyone on the island said Red Feather was the wildest stallion in the herd. Some even nicknamed him, "Crazy Horse". Can you guess why?

But Red Feather wasn't crazy—he just liked adventure.
Red Feather was very smart. He was also very curious.
He was not afraid of people. He could not resist
going into yards and eating the tasty green grass.
He especially loved to nibble on flowers. But nothing
was more fun than tipping over trash cans on garbage
day. This made lots of people mad. They chased him
out of their yards, shouting, "Go away, you garbage
thief!"

Eating morsels out of garbage cans gave Red Feather his first taste of apples. Red Feather loved apples. Sometimes children would toss him an apple. Whenever Red Feather saw children, he looked for an apple.

One day, he followed some children to the supermarket. When the children came out of the market eating apples, Red Feather learned a lesson. Apples came from supermarkets—not kids! After that day, Red Feather was a regular supermarket customer. When the automatic door opened, Red Feather rushed inside. Then he zigzagged through the store, bypassing the men who tried to shoo him away, while the customers laughed.

"Why, if I didn't know better," said the manager, "I'd swear that hoss had a smile on his face!"

Red Feather was making a name for himself in Corolla. Both the locals and the tourists loved him. He enjoyed the attention they gave him—as long as they didn't come too close.

He loved his home in Corolla. But sometimes he longed to see other places. One morning, Red Feather decided to take a trip. He rounded up his family of mares and headed north. Everything was grand—until they came to a tall fence that blocked the way. Red Feather snorted in disgust. Then he reared high and pawed the air with his hooves. He trotted up and down the fence line looking for an opening, but there was none. Still, Red Feather would not give up. There had to be a way around that fence. After all, ...

...adventure was calling him!

He trotted along the fence until he came to the place where the land ended and the ocean began.

Stopping at the water's edge he looked back at his mares. Would they follow him into the scary waters?

Luckily, horses can swim. Red Feather did not dilly-dally. He plunged into the surf, his mares right behind him. The waves were strong, but Red Feather was determined. Around the fence they swam. They scrambled up on the other side and shook themselves dry. Red Feather sniffed the air. "Let's go," he whinnied. "Adventure awaits!" The little band followed Red Feather as he traveled across a narrow land bridge into Virginia.

They had not gone far when they surprised some people on the beach. Although they were wild horses, they were used to tourists on the beaches of Corolla in the summertime.

Soon they found a patch of sea oats. Munching and crunching, they forgot about the people on the beach. Until...

"Va-room! Va-room!"

All of the horses had seen cars and trucks before. But this one was different. It had a big boxy thing attached to it.

The truck stopped a short distance from the horses. Men got out of the truck. Red Feather was not afraid, but his eyes followed their every move.

The men did not come toward the horses. Instead, they started setting up a portable corral.

When the corral was finished, the men surrounded the horses and drove them into the corral and then into the trailer. Although Red Feather was annoyed, he did not put up much of a fight. Here was a new adventure!

At first, all of the horses were scared. But they soon discovered that riding in the trailer was fun.

They traveled for what seemed like a long time before the truck stopped.

Red Feather sniffed the air. It smelled familiar— pine trees and salty sea scents.

They were home again!

After that adventure, Red Feather and his band became regulars on the Virginia side of the fence. But every time they went to Virginia, the men with the trailer came and carried them back to Corolla.

That did not stop Red Feather's adventures. Instead, with each trip Red Feather grew smarter.

He soon learned that while the men unloaded the corral panels, he and his mares had plenty of time to escape.

This game was fun!

Of all the mares in his band, Cinnamon was his favorite. One brisk April morn Cinnamon appeared with a newborn colt. Red Feather pranced and kicked up his heels. He nuzzled the colt, then trotted around the dunes proudly.

The colt grew fast. He was smart and quick like his daddy, but looked like his mama.

As the days grew short and cool, food became scarce. Red Feather remembered the sea oats on the other side of the fence. He decided to take his family north again. There were now five mares in his band. Each mare had a colt.

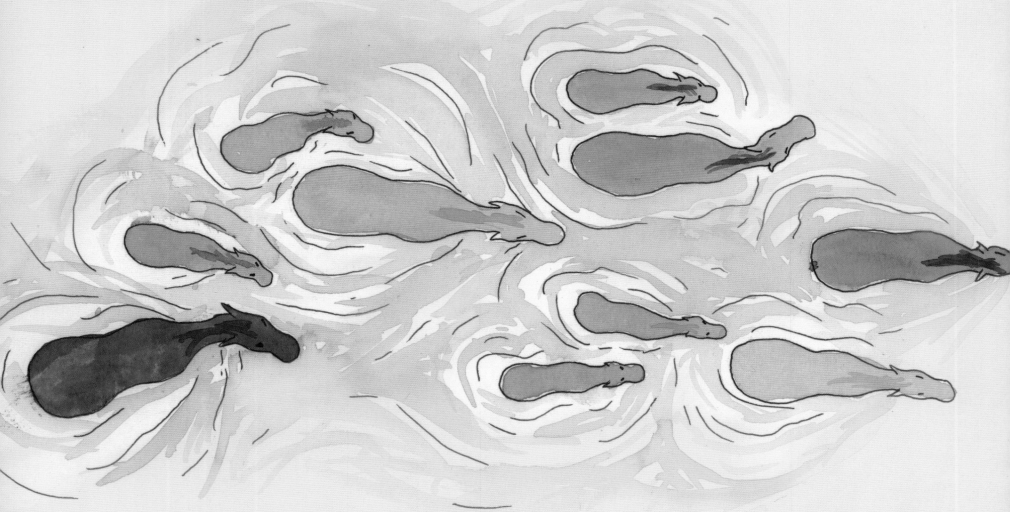

Luckily, even little colts can swim.

This time, Red Feather pushed his band farther north than ever before.

They traveled to the village of Sandbridge looking for food. Instead of dirt paths, there were hard-paved roads.

Cars in Sandbridge were not used to having horses walk across their roads.

In a screech of tires a colt dropped to the ground. It was Cinnamon's baby. The tiny colt was writhing in pain and had a large gash on his hip.

Red Feather jumped into action. He raced to his colt, teeth bared and ears flattened against his head.

The people in the car climbed out to see what had happened.

With a wild stallion standing guard, no one dared approach the colt.

Soon, a man and woman arrived with a horse trailer. They unloaded fence panels and built a portable corral. This time, Red Feather did not try to escape.

When the corral was finished, he gingerly stepped over his colt and drove the mares into the pen. Then he allowed the man to touch his baby and dress the colt's wound.

That night, the trailer carried Red Feather and his mares away. But the little colt was left behind. Red Feather knew that his baby needed human help, but he still wanted to be with him. Inside the trailer, he kicked and fought, but he could not escape. He would have to wait until he got back to Corolla.

All night he stayed awake pacing up and down trying to decide what to do.

Before the sun rose the next morning, Red Feather swam around the ocean fence one more time. He had to find his baby!

When Red Feather arrived at the accident site, there was no sign of his son or the trailer or the man and woman. Red Feather pranced up and down the highway, looking for clues.

By sundown, Red Feather stood with his head hanging down. He nickered sadly.

He was about to start back home when he heard the familiar sound of the noisy truck barreling down the beach. He whinnied and trotted to meet the truck.

After the truck stopped, the man and woman got out. "Did you come back to check on your baby?" the woman asked.

Red Feather nickered.

"We'll take you to him," the man said.

At the veterinary clinic, Red Feather followed a shrill whinny to one of the horse pens. "Just look," said the woman. "Red Feather's happy to see his baby."

And he was. The stallion sniffed his colt from head to hoof, just to make sure he was all right.

"I think you've had enough adventure,"
the woman said, smiling.

Red Feather neighed and nodded his head. And
he never swam around the ocean fence again.

The True Story of Red Feather

When my Red Feather was captured by the new herd manager at the Corolla Wild Horse Fund he was mistakenly thought to be THE Red Feather. Later it was learned that he is the son of the famous Red Feather. Like his father, his wanderlust placed him and his mares in great danger.

Though he looks like a teddy bear, he is the most athletic horse with whom I have ever shared a round pen. He was once hot tempered and ready to fight at the drop of a hat and now he is simply a sweet little horse just looking for a hug or a scratch.

A rodeo cowboy from out west rode my little Red Feather one day. He was used to riding and working big horses. After he rode Red Feather all that he had to say was that he was the smoothest moving horse that he had ever ridden.

This book is a great mixture of stories about my Red Feather and his famous father and all of the great horses of Corolla.

Steve Edwards

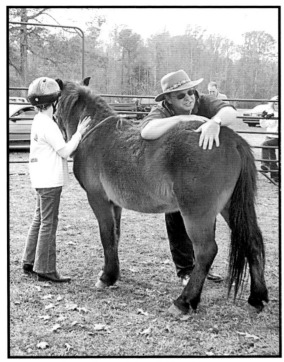

Steve Edwards and Red Feather at a Natural Horsemanship Clinic

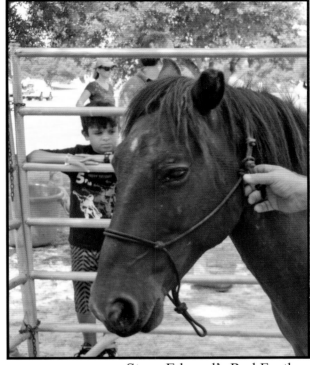

Steve Edward's Red Feather

A Note from the Author:

There are really two wild horses named Red Feather from Corolla (pronounced, "Co-raw-la") named Red Feather. Both are rescued horses. This story is a blending of tales that surround these two colorful stallions. Today, they both lead happy lives in the safety of civilization. But for the remainder of their relatives—those mustangs that still roam wild on the Outer Banks of North Carolina—life is not so easy. These horses are descendants of the mustangs that were brought to the New World in the sixteenth century by Spanish explorers. Today, their very existence is threatened. In 1989, a group of concerned volunteers founded the Corolla Wild Horse Fund, a non-profit organization whose mission is to care for and protect these American historical treasures.

To learn more more about these noble steeds and how you can help them continue to live wild and free, please contact the Corolla Wild Horse Fund.

COROLLA WILD HORSE FUND
INCORPORATED

The Corolla Wild Horse Fund
Karen McCalpin, Director
P.O. Box 361
1126 Old Schoolhouse Lane
Corolla, North Carolina 27927
(252) 453-8002
E-mail: info@corollawildhorses.com
www.corollawildhorses.com

About the Author

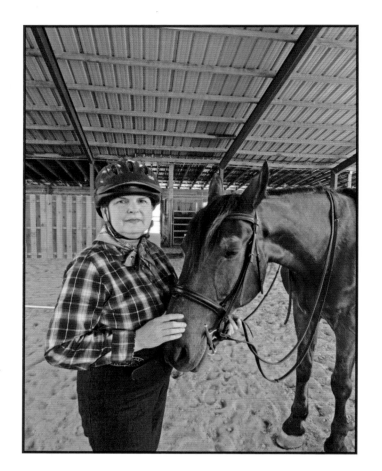

Linda Whittington Hurst is an award winning author who currently resides in Lake Charles, Louisiana where she is an assistant professor at McNeese State University. In 2011, Linda won the Pinnacle Award for Excellence in Teaching. This award afforded her both the time and the resources to complete this book. She is cofounder of the Southwest Louisiana Children's Book Writers and Illustrators Guild.

Linda has always loved horses, books and teaching. Writing stories about horses is one of her favorite pastimes. Although she shares a concern for the fate of wild horses worldwide, she is particularly passionate about the future of the Colonial Spanish Mustangs of Corolla, North Carolina, which are featured in several of her books.

About the Illustrator

Erin Casteel is a native of Sulphur, Louisiana. She is an art teacher, illustrator, local mural painter, and "Ignorance Is Bliss" comic strip creator. She is a charter member of Southwest Louisiana Children's Book Writers and Illustrators Guild.

As a professional artist, she has participated in numerous community art shows. This is her first published book.

Wild Pony Press
© 2011
ISBN – 978-0-615-49695-5